Dear Parent:
Your child's love of reading starts here!

Every child learns to read in a different way and at his or her own speed. Some go back and forth between reading levels and read favorite books again and again. Others read through each level in order. You can help your young reader improve and become more confident by encouraging his or her own interests and abilities. From books your child reads with you to the first books he or she reads alone, there are I Can Read Books for every stage of reading:

SHARED READING
Basic language, word repetition, and whimsical illustrations, ideal for sharing with your emergent reader

BEGINNING READING
Short sentences, familiar words, and simple concepts for children eager to read on their own

READING WITH HELP
Engaging stories, longer sentences, and language play for developing readers

READING ALONE
Complex plots, challenging vocabulary, and high-interest topics for the independent reader

ADVANCED READING
Short paragraphs, chapters, and exciting themes for the perfect bridge to chapter books

I Can Read Books have introduced children to the joy of reading since 1957. Featuring award-winning authors and illustrators and a fabulous cast of beloved characters, I Can Read Books set the standard for beginning readers.

A lifetime of discovery begins with the magical words **"I Can Read!"**

Visit www.icanread.com for information
on enriching your child's reading experience.

I Can Read Book® is a trademark of HarperCollins Publishers.

Happy Go Ducky
Copyright © 2012 by Jackie Urbanovic. Manufactured in China. No part of this book may be used or reproduced in any manner whatsoever without written permission except in the case of brief quotations embodied in critical articles and reviews. For information address HarperCollins Children's Books, a division of HarperCollins Publishers, 10 East 53rd Street, New York, NY 10022.
www.icanread.com
Library of Congress catalog card number: 2011929312
ISBN 978-0-06-186440-7 (trade bdg.)—ISBN 978-0-06-186439-1 (pbk.)
Design by Sean Boggs

12   13   14   15   16   SCP   10   9   8   7   6   5   4   3   2   1   ❖   First Edition

I Can Read!

BEGINNING
1
READING

HAPPY GO DUCKY

based on the bestselling books by
Jackie Urbanovic
cover illustration by Jackie Urbanovic
story by Lori Haskins Houran
pictures by Joe Mathieu

HARPER
An Imprint of HarperCollinsPublishers

Max was happy.

TOO happy.

He stared at the sky

with a strange grin on his face.

"Smell the flowers!" he said.

"Feel the breeze!"

"What's with him?" asked Coco.

"Spring fever," said Bebe.

"Today is the first day of spring."

Coco waved a paw in front of Max.

He didn't blink.

"Will he be like this all day?"

Coco asked.

"All day," said Bebe.

Coco and Bebe went inside.

Irene came out.

"I'm leaving for the day, Max.

You're in charge, okay?"

"Okay," said Max

in a dreamy voice.

Irene told Max what to do.

MAIL.... SWEEP. SCRUB.
PLANT.. DISHES .TRASH
.GRASS.KITTENS...

As soon as Irene left, Max got started.

Coco looked out the window.

"Bebe?" she said.

"Why is Max sweeping the grass?"

Max dragged the hose inside.

"Sweep the grass," he said.

"Water the floor."

"Oh, no!" said Bebe.

"It's Irene's day away.

Guess who she left in charge?"

Max turned on the hose.

"ACK!" yelled Coco.

She grabbed the hose and shut it off.

Max wandered away.

"What do we do?" cried Bebe.

"We have to undo everything

Max does," Coco said.

"Starting with this mess!"

Meanwhile, Max was busy.
"Take out the dishes,"
he said.

"Put away the trash."

"Mail the salad.

Toss the letters.

Plant the laundry.

Hang the seeds."

Coco and Bebe ran around all day
fixing Max's mix-ups.

"What's Max up to now?"

asked Coco.

Bebe peeked in the kitchen window.

"He has some potatoes," said Bebe.

"I think he's trying to feed

the potatoes the kittens' food!"

"FEED the potatoes?" said Coco.

Coco and Bebe got the giggles.

They rolled around on the grass.

Suddenly Bebe sat up.

"Wait a second.

What was Max supposed

to do to the potatoes?"

"I don't know," said Coco.

"Chop them? Peel them?"

Then she gasped.

"THE KITTENS!"

Coco and Bebe ran into the house.

"MAX! STOP!" they yelled.

Max stood in front of the sink.

The kittens were inside the sink,

playing with soap bubbles.

"Scrub the kittens," said Max.

Then he blinked.

"Scrub the kittens?" he said.

Max looked around.
He saw the kittens
covered with soap.
He saw the potatoes
covered with cat food.

Just then Irene walked in.

"Nice job today, Max!

Everything looks great.

You're even giving

the kittens a bath? Wow!"

Irene looked over at Coco and Bebe.

They had strange grins on their faces.

"SCRUB, not chop!" said Coco.

"SCRUB, not peel!" said Bebe.

"What's with them?" asked Irene.

"And what's with the potatoes
in the cat food?"

"I think I know," said Max.

"Spring fever!"